When Katie's Parents Separated

By Sarah, Duchess of York

Illustrated by Ian Cunliffe

STERLING

New York / London

STERLING and the distinctive Sterling logo are registered trademarks of
Sterling Publishing Co., Inc.

Library of Congress Cataloging-in-Publication Data Available

Lot #:
2 4 6 8 10 9 7 5 3 1
10/10
Published by Sterling Publishing Co., Inc.
387 Park Avenue South, New York, NY 10016
Story and illustrations © 2007 by Startworks Ltd.
"Ten Helpful Hints" © 2009 by Startworks Ltd.
Distributed in Canada by Sterling Publishing
c/o Canadian Manda Group, 165 Dufferin Street
Toronto, Ontario, Canada M6K 3H6
Distributed in Australia by Capricorn Link (Australia) Pty. Ltd.
P.O. Box 704, Windsor, NSW 2756, Australia

Sterling ISBN 978-1-4027-7395-2

For information about custom editions, special sales, premium and
corporate purchases, please contact Sterling Special Sales
Department at 800-805-5489 or specialsales@sterlingpublishing.com.

All children face many new experiences as they grow up, and helping them to understand and deal with each is one of the most demanding and rewarding things we do as parents. Helping Hand Books are for both children and parents to read, perhaps together. Each simple story describes a childhood experience and shows some of the ways in which to make it a positive one. I do hope these books encourage children and parents to talk about these sometimes difficult issues. Talking together goes a long way to finding a solution.

Sarah,

Sarah, Duchess of York

Mornings were always the worst.

Katie woke up with an empty feeling again. Then she remembered—her dad was no longer living with them.

A few months ago, Katie's parents told her that her dad was going to live somewhere else. They said that they did not want to be married anymore. But they promised her that they both still loved her very much.

Then they gave her two lockets. One held a picture of her mom and the other held a picture of her dad.

"So you can be with both of us all the time," her dad explained.

Katie thought this meant she would not see her dad anymore. But Dad quickly explained she would stay with him every other weekend and some holidays, too. He said they would do lots of things together.

Katie thought about what had happened since that day. She and her mom had moved from their house into an apartment five miles away.

Katie soon learned to love her new bedroom. She also made two good friends, David and Megan, who lived on the same street.

Katie helped with some of the chores around the apartment. After dinner one night, her mom called her "My Right-Hand Girl," which made Katie feel very important.

She loved the way her mom smiled now and made silly jokes again. There was no more of the arguing that went on when her mom and dad were together.

Weekends with her dad were good, too. He loved to cook, so mealtimes were great. Katie also got to sleep in a brand new bunk bed.

Her dad always planned something fun. One day they went for a walk in the park to feed the ducks. Another weekend they went to the movies. Her dad even bought them popcorn!

"So why do I still feel sad about Mom and Dad?" Katie asked herself one morning.

She got out of bed and joined her mom for breakfast.

"I've got good news!" said Katie's mom. "Aunt Meredith is letting us use her house for a week while she is away in August.

"It's near the mountains and by a lake. We can take walks and go swimming. And there's room for three, so you can bring one of your friends."

Katie was thrilled! She loved to swim. But there were two friends she wanted to bring along.

"Megan is my best friend so I should pick her, but she's not really a good swimmer. Grace loves swimming, but I don't want to upset Megan. Mom, what should I do? Who should I invite?"

"I don't know, sweetie. I'm sure you'll figure it out," said her mom.

The next weekend Katie went to stay with her dad.

They were taking a walk through the park when her dad said, "I would like to take you on a summer vacation, just you and me. How about going camping?"

"That sounds great! Will we sleep in a tent?" asked Katie.

"That's usually how we do it!" said her dad with a smile.

"Can I bring a friend?" asked Katie.

"No, it will be just the two of us," replied Dad.

"But Mom is letting me bring a friend on our summer vacation," Katie said.

"Then you're a very lucky girl, having two summer vacations," said Dad. "This vacation will be just you and me."

That evening, Katie was back at home with her mom.

"Why can't we all go on vacation together anymore?" Katie asked curiously. "Is it because of me?"

"Of course not, Katie," said her mom. "It's just that your dad and I find it better to be apart. It is not your fault. We both want to be with you because we love you so much."

That night, Katie lay in bed thinking. It always upset her a little when she left her mom to be with her dad. Then again, she was sad to leave her dad when she came back to stay with her mom.

It felt like having to choose between two very important people, like she had to do with Megan and Grace.

But Katie also saw that her mom and dad seemed happier now. Maybe in time she would stop missing her old life and fully enjoy things about her new life.

Katie held both lockets in her hand. She looked at the pictures of her parents for a long time. In each photo, her parents were smiling back at her.

"I may have two homes, and everything is a bit different now," she thought. "But there are good things about my new life, too. The very best part is that my parents love me and they always will. That will never change. Families come in all shapes and sizes, and mine is going to be just right for all of us."

TEN HELPFUL HINTS

FOR PARENTS WHO HAVE SEPARATED

By Dr. Richard Woolfson, PhD

1. As soon as you can, explain to your child what is going on. If she asks difficult questions, give honest answers that are suitable to her age and level of understanding. Reinforce the idea that you both still love her very much.

2. Have confidence in your parenting skills. Don't assume that you have to overcompensate because your child doesn't have two parents at home any more. It is very possible to thrive in a one-parent household.

3. Resist the temptation to spoil him. Do not feel uncomfortable about continuing to set limits and boundaries. Every child needs a clear structure at home, set within a loving framework.

4. Arrange contact between your child and your ex. Do what you can to ensure there are regular visits between your child and your former partner. Although this can be emotionally challenging for you, it is in her best interest.

5. Strike a balance between parenting and sharing. You might want to be his friend and comfort him through this difficult time. That is fine, but you are also his parent and should still be managing his behavior. Also, try not to burden your child with your own worries.

6. Accept emotional and practical help when it is offered. Taking help from friends and relatives is not a sign of weakness nor does it mean you are an inadequate parent. Be prepared to accept practical support from your former partner, too, if it's offered.

7. Don't try to be two parents. If you feel single parenting is getting to be too much for you, seek advice and support from friends and family. Have realistic expectations.

8. Don't use your child as an emotional weapon. Keep her out of all battles between you and your former partner. Don't use her as a way of getting back at your ex, and make sure your ex doesn't do it either. Your child needs to see a settled relationship between the two of you.

9. Remember that your child wants to remain loyal to both parents. Avoid pushing him into choosing sides between the two of you. No matter how much anger you might feel toward your former partner, the fact is that your child loves both of you.

10. Prepare for the future. Circumstances change and people move on with their lives. You and your ex are likely to find new partners. Recognize that this could be difficult for your child to accept and approach any new relationships with care.

Dr. Richard Woolfson is a child psychologist, working with children and their families. He is also an author and has written several books on child development and family life, in addition to numerous articles for magazines and newspapers. Dr. Woolfson runs training workshops for parents and child care professionals and appears regularly on radio and television. He is a Fellow of the British Psychological Society.

Helping Hand Books

Look for these other helpful books to share with your child: